The Fourth
Pony Pal

Do you love ponies? Be a Pony Pal!

PONY PALS

The Fourth Pony Pal

Jeanne Betancourt

Illustrated by Paul Bachem

A
LITTLE APPLE
PAPERBACK

SCHOLASTIC INC.

New York   Toronto   London   Auckland   Sydney
Mexico City   New Delhi   Hong Kong   Buenos Aires

ISBN 0-439-30643-4

SCHOLASTIC, LITTLE APPLE PAPERBACKS, and associated logos are trademarks and/or registered trademarks of Scholastic Inc.

12 11 10 9 8 7 6 5 4 3 2 1   2 3 4 5 6/0

Printed in the U.S.A.   40
First Scholastic printing, January 2002

Contents

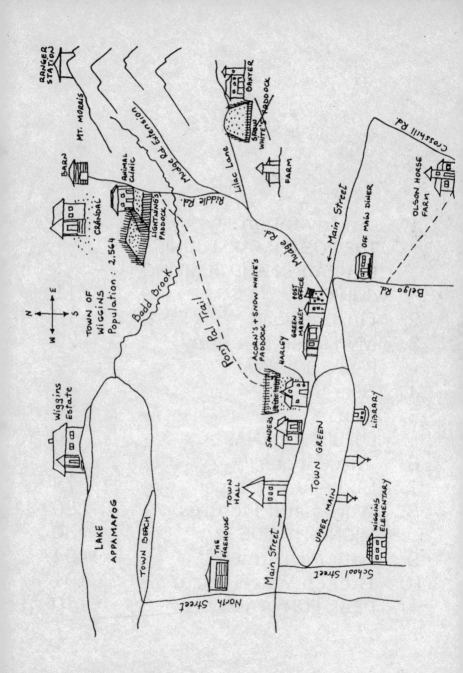

The Fourth
Pony Pal

An Invitation

Anna Harley and Lulu Sanders went to their ponies' paddock after school. When Anna's brown-and-black Shetland pony saw her, he ran in the other direction.

Lulu laughed. "Acorn loves to tease you," she said.

"I like to tease him, too," said Anna. "Watch this."

Anna turned and walked back toward her house. Acorn whinnied as if to say, "Where are you going?" Anna swung around and held up a carrot.

Acorn trotted to the paddock gate and waited for her.

Meanwhile, Lulu's pony, Snow White, cantered over to the gate for her carrot.

"I missed you today," Lulu told Snow White. "I miss you every day I go to school. Next week we have vacation. We'll be together all day, every day."

"We'll go on long trail rides and have barn sleepovers," added Anna as she gave Acorn his carrot.

Acorn's ears went forward. He turned suddenly and ran to the far end of the paddock. "He heard something," said Anna.

"Probably a deer in the woods," observed Lulu.

Acorn hadn't heard a deer. He'd heard a pony and rider. It was Pam Crandal riding her pony, Lightning, on Pony Pal Trail. The mile-and-a-half woodland trail connected the Crandals' property to Acorn and Snow White's paddock. Pam moved Lightning into a gallop. She couldn't wait to see her Pony Pals. She had big news.

As Pam rode off the trail, Lightning whinnied a hello to Acorn.

Anna, Lulu, and Snow White ran to meet the surprise visitors.

"I thought you had to do your homework," Lulu called to Pam.

"I do," said Pam, "but something happened. Something we have to talk about right away."

"What?" asked Anna and Lulu in unison.

Pam dismounted and led Lightning into the paddock.

"There's an equitation clinic in Virginia," she began excitedly. "Eleanor Morgan, my mom's friend — "

"We know Eleanor," said Lulu. "She won the bronze medal for show jumping in the Olympics."

"Right," said Pam as she unbuckled Lightning's girth. "So Eleanor got me a place in the clinic. It's hard to get into and there's lots of jumping. The woman who runs it is named Mrs. Foster. Her daughter, Shelly, was going to be in the clinic. But she's

dropped out so there's this extra spot."

Anna took off Lightning's bridle. "When is it?" she asked.

"Next week," said Pam. "During our vacation."

Anna was disappointed. The Pony Pals wouldn't be together during vacation.

Lulu helped Pam take off Lightning's saddle. "We'll miss you," she said. "But you should still go."

Pam grinned. "You don't have to miss me," she said. "You can come. Eleanor got us all invited. Snow White and Acorn, too. My mother said she'd drive us down with the horse trailer."

"We got into the clinic!" said Lulu, surprised. "I thought there was only one empty place."

"You wouldn't *be* in the clinic," explained Pam. "Mrs. Foster said you could come as observers." Pam hesitated. "We might have more fun staying in Wiggins."

"It's a big deal to go to a clinic like that,"

said Lulu. "You and Lightning are terrific at jumping."

Pam looked worried. "I don't know if I want to go. I might not be as good as the other riders."

Anna and Lulu exchanged a glance. They both had the same idea.

"We'd better have a Pony Pal meeting," Lulu told Pam.

"Let's go to my house," suggested Anna.

A few minutes later, the three girls were sitting at the Harley kitchen table. Anna passed around a plate of cookies. Lulu poured out glasses of juice.

"The big problem," said Pam, "is that we're not *all* in the clinic."

"I wouldn't want to be in the clinic, anyway," said Anna. "Acorn and I would rather trail ride."

"Anna and I can hang out together while you have classes," said Lulu. "Even if Anna and I don't go, you should go."

Pam shook her head. "I won't go without you."

Anna and Lulu looked at each other. It was up to them. Lulu nodded.

Anna smiled. "We all should go," she said. "It'll be a Pony Pal vacation."

"A Pony Pal adventure," added Lulu.

"Eleanor said there are some great trails around the farm," Pam told them. "Maybe Shelly Foster will take you on rides."

Lulu reached for a cookie. "I wonder why Shelly isn't doing the clinic," she said.

"Maybe she was hurt riding," guessed Anna. "Which means she won't be able to ride with us, either."

That night, Pam lay in bed thinking about the clinic. Lightning loves jumping. She'll have a good time at the clinic. But will Anna and Lulu? wondered Pam. Will I? She turned and pulled the blanket over her head.

Lulu had on her pajamas, but she wasn't in bed yet. She looked out the window at her pony. Snow White's coat shone in the moonlight. I've never put Snow White in a horse trailer or gone to a new place with her, she thought. What if Snow White doesn't like the trailer? What if she's afraid? Snow White has already had some bad experiences.

The day Lulu found the pretty white pony, her leg was caught in barbed wire. Another time, Snow White was lost in a snowstorm and trapped in a big icy hole. Would the trip to Virginia be another bad experience for Snow White?

Lulu crawled between the covers and lay back on her pillow. At least Snow White will be with her pals, she thought. No matter what happens on our trip, we'll all be together.

Anna sat up in bed looking at her photo album of Acorn. There were pictures of Acorn in costumes when he was in the circus. In another photo he was leading a parade down Main Street. There were pictures of Acorn in a movie. Acorn is a star, thought Anna. He's used to being the center of attention. But he won't be a star at the clinic. We're not even in the clinic.

Anna closed the album. She had painted

Acorn's head on the cover. Anna loved the way Acorn's eyes sparkled in the painting. She put the album on her nightstand and turned out the light. I hope Acorn has a good time on our vacation, she thought.

As Anna curled up under the covers, a new idea popped into her head. It was the first time the Pony Pals were going on a trip out of Wiggins. Three girls and three ponies. We'll have a great time, decided Anna. Nothing is going to go wrong.

Fax

To: Pam Crandal

From: Eleanor Morgan

Pages: 6

Dear Pam,

I am so pleased that you — and your Pony Pals — are going to the Foster Farm and that you will be in the clinic. It will be good for you to work with Mrs. Foster. She is one of the top instructors on the East Coast. Don't be nervous about anything. I've seen you ride and jump. You're good. That's why I recommended you. Anna and Lulu will have fun meeting new people and riding in the Virginia hills. It's gorgeous country and warmer than Wiggins at this time of year. I've attached the information about the clinic. Say hi to Anna and Lulu for me. And, of course, Lightning.

Love,
Eleanor

THE FOSTER FARM
JUNIOR EQUITATION
AND JUMPING CLINIC

*A clinic that takes you
and your horse to new heights and
into the winner's circle!*

WHAT TO EXPECT
AT OUR RIDING CLINIC

- ♘ To take care of your own horse
- ♘ To ride and jump better every day
- ♘ To make friends with other riders
- ♘ To do your personal best for yourself
  and your horse

DAILY SCHEDULE
Monday–Friday

7:00 A.M.	Rise and shine
7:30	Feed horses
8:00	Breakfast
9:00–10:30	Class 1: Flat work
10:30–11:30	Horse care
12–1 P.M.	Lunch
1–3:30	Class 2: Jumping
3:30	Snack
4–6	Barn chores and free time
6–7	Dinner
7–9	Video screenings and guest lectures
9:30	Lights-out

WHAT TO BRING FOR YOUR HORSE

- Saddle pad
- Saddle
- Bridle
- Extra lead rope and halter
- Blanket
- Grooming box
- First aid kit
- Buckets
- Hay and grain

WHAT TO BRING FOR YOURSELF

- Sleeping bag
- Hard hat
- Barn clothes
- Riding clothes
- Pants and riding jacket
- Boots

"*I learned more in a one-week clinic at Foster Farm than I did in a year of lessons at home.*"

— Kristen Roth

"*Foster's is a super riding clinic. It's the best. I love it.*"

— Brooke O'Hanolan

"*My competition record has really improved. Now I win blue ribbons all the time. Thank you, Mrs. Foster.*"

— Aviva Granger

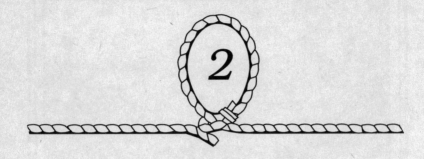

On the Road

Pam and her father put her suitcase, sleeping bag, saddle, and tack trunk in the back of the pickup truck. "You sure you didn't forget anything?" he asked.

"I checked everything on the list twice," she told him.

"A whole week without Pam," said her father. "I'll miss you, honey."

"I'll miss you, too, Dad," she said. Pam looked around at the house, barns, and fields. Her father was a veterinarian and her mother was a riding teacher. There were always interesting animals and people at the Crandals'. She'd miss it all.

Pam's mother walked over to them. "Ready?" she asked.

"I just have to get Lightning," answered Pam. Pam ran to the barn. "Hey, girl," she called to her pony. "Let's go."

Lightning followed Pam to the back of the horse trailer and walked right in. Pam tied Lightning's lead rope to the inside of the trailer.

"Your friends will be in here soon," Pam told her pony as she closed the trailer door.

A few minutes later Mrs. Crandal and Pam waved good-bye to Dr. Crandal and drove onto Riddle Road.

Anna and Lulu stood on Anna's front porch next to two tack trunks, two saddles, two suitcases, and two sleeping bags.

"Are you sure we didn't forget anything?" asked Lulu.

Anna looked over at the pile. She had a strange feeling that something was missing. "My art supplies!" she exclaimed.

Anna ran inside and up to her room. A red knapsack packed with sketchbooks, colored pencils, watercolors, and brushes was on her desk. Pam and Lulu were bringing their journals to write about the trip. Anna was going to draw and paint pictures in her journal. Anna was dyslexic, so she had trouble with writing and reading. But she was a terrific artist. She grabbed her knapsack and ran back down the stairs.

Anna added her knapsack to the pile on the front porch.

"Here comes my grandmother," Lulu told her.

Lulu's grandmother was walking across the lawn toward the Harleys. Grandmother Sanders's house was next to the Harley house. Lulu's mother died when Lulu was little. Her father was a naturalist who traveled all over the world studying wild animals and their environments. Lulu used to travel with her father, but now she lived in Wiggins with her grandmother. Her father lived there, too, in between his trips.

Grandmother Sanders came up the porch steps. She was carrying three identical pink plastic bags. She handed Lulu one of the bags. "I've brought you all presents," she explained. "For your trip." She handed the other two bags to Anna. "One is for Pam."

"Thank you," said Anna and Lulu in unison.

"What's in it?" Anna asked as she unzipped the bag.

"Shampoo, cream rinse, soap, nail files, comb, brush, and hand lotion," said Grandmother Sanders proudly. "Use the lotion morning and night." Lulu's grandmother was a hairdresser and owned a beauty salon. She was always giving the Pony Pals grooming tips.

Lulu gave her grandmother a big hug and said thank you again.

Anna looked at her watch. "Pam and her mother are going to be here any minute," she said. "It's time to get Acorn and Snow White."

When Anna and Lulu came back with their ponies, the pickup truck with the horse trailer was parked in front of the house. Anna's mother and Lulu's grandmother were helping Mrs. Crandal load Anna's and Lulu's things into the truck.

When Pam opened the trailer doors, Lightning whinnied a hello to Acorn and Snow White.

Acorn sniffed around the trailer door. Snow White backed away from it.

"It's okay, Snow White," said Lulu. "You're going to be with your friends."

"I'll go in first with Acorn," offered Anna. Acorn was curious about the trailer and followed Anna right in.

"Come on, Snow White," Lulu said in a soothing voice. She gave a little tug to the lead rope. Snow White stepped carefully into the trailer. Lulu led her to the space next to Acorn.

Acorn turned and sniffed Snow White's face. Lightning nickered gently. Snow White nodded and whinnied as if to say, "If you are both here, I guess it's okay."

The girls left the trailer, and Pam closed the door.

Anna's mother handed Pam a picnic basket and Anna a big box tied with a red ribbon. "I packed you all supper for the road," she said. "And brownies for you to give Mrs. Foster." Anna's mother owned the only diner in Wiggins. She made exceptional chewy brownies. "There are brownies in your picnic basket, too," she added with a grin.

"So we're all set," said Mrs. Crandal. "Let's get this show on the road."

The three girls climbed into the truck. Lulu and Anna sat in the back. Pam sat up front with her mother.

Mrs. Harley leaned into the truck and gave Anna a kiss good-bye. "I'll miss you, sweetie," she said.

Anna felt a lump in her throat. She was already a little homesick.

The pickup truck pulled the horse trailer down Main Street and out of Wiggins.

"Good-bye, Wiggins," Lulu shouted out the window.

"We're taking our ponies on a trip," yelled Pam.

"We're on vacation!" added Anna. "No school for a week."

Pam turned around and hit high fives with her friends. "All right!" they shouted in unison.

Lulu loved that they were going on a trip. "Traveling is so much fun!" she exclaimed. "I've never been to Virginia."

Mrs. Crandal told the girls that they would see a lot of horses in Virginia. "And beautiful horse farms," she added.

After driving for two hours, they stopped to have their picnic. Then they got back in the truck and drove for another two hours.

The closer they came to Virginia, the more Pam worried about the clinic. "There are five other riders in the clinic," she said. "I bet they're all older than me."

"So what?" asked Anna. "Older kids don't scare you. Besides, you said Shelly is our age."

"But she's not in the clinic," Pam pointed out.

For a while everyone was quiet. Anna leaned her head on Lulu's shoulder and closed her eyes. She wondered why Shelly dropped out of the clinic and what she would be like.

The next thing Anna knew, Lulu was patting her cheek. "Anna, wake up," she said. "We're almost there."

Anna sat up and looked out the window. They were driving past a beautiful horse farm. At every turn in the road there was another farm with horses, barns, and a large house.

"I like Virginia so far," said Lulu.

Soon, they came to a red-and-gold sign that read FOSTER HORSE FARM. Anna thought the farm looked fancier than in the brochure.

"It's so big," observed Lulu.

"They have a lot of horses," added Pam.

"And a really cute pony," said Anna. She pointed out the window. "See the palomino in with those four horses."

"That's the only pony I see," commented Pam.

"Maybe there are more ponies in the barn," said Lulu.

Pam wondered if she'd be the only rider in the clinic with a pony.

My Horse Is a Pony

Mrs. Crandal stopped the truck next to the barn and the Pony Pals climbed out.

Anna stretched her arms and twirled. "It's so beautiful here!" she exclaimed. "I love it."

A woman dressed in riding clothes came out of the barn. "Welcome!" she said, smiling. "I'm Regina Foster."

Mrs. Foster shook hands with Mrs. Crandal and each of the girls introduced herself.

"Let's get your horses out of the trailer," said Mrs. Foster. "They could probably use a good run."

"They're not horses, they're —" Anna began. But Mrs. Foster wasn't listening to Anna. She was busy talking to Mrs. Crandal.

As the girls led their ponies out of the trailer, Snow White nuzzled Lulu's shoulder. "You're a good pony," said Lulu. "I'm proud of you."

Pam scratched Lightning's upside-down heart for good luck. I'll need it for the clinic, she thought.

Acorn looked around boldly and sniffed the fresh air. "It's very fancy here, Acorn," Anna told him. "We're going to have fun."

While the girls put their ponies in the field, Mrs. Crandal drove the trailer behind the barn. Mrs. Foster helped her unhitch it from the pickup truck.

The ponies ran freely in a big field.

Snow White is not acting afraid, thought Lulu. She'll be okay here.

Next, the girls unloaded their suitcases, sleeping bags, pony supplies, and saddles from the truck.

Mrs. Foster and Mrs. Crandal helped them

put the tack trunks and saddles in the tack room. Lulu thought Mrs. Foster was very kind. She even invited Mrs. Crandal to stay overnight.

"Thanks, but I'm staying with a friend," Mrs. Crandal explained. "She lives about halfway toward home." Mrs. Crandal looked at her watch. "I'd better leave now or I'll be driving all night."

Mrs. Crandal hugged each of the girls, ending with Pam. "I know you and Lightning will learn a lot, honey," she said. "You're in good hands with Mrs. Foster." She smiled at Anna and Lulu. "Have a great time."

"Thanks for driving us, Mrs. Crandal," said Lulu.

Mrs. Crandal turned the truck around and headed down the driveway.

As Pam waved good-bye to her mother, she wondered where the other girls in the clinic were.

Lulu noticed that Mrs. Foster's friendly smile disappeared as soon as Mrs. Crandal was gone.

Where is Shelly Foster? wondered Anna.

"All right, you three," said Mrs. Foster. "Grab your suitcases and sleeping bags and we'll go into the house. The other girls are already settling into their rooms."

"When we stay over at Pam's we sleep in the barn," said Anna cheerfully. "We call ourselves the Pony Pals and love to trail ride."

Mrs. Foster wasn't paying any attention to Anna. She was watching a skinny, short-haired girl walking toward the house. The girl had on a Walkman and snapped her fingers to music no one else could hear.

"Shelly!" Mrs. Foster shouted as she ran toward the girl. "I've been looking all over for you."

The Pony Pals tried to keep up with Mrs. Foster, but they couldn't. Their suitcases and sleeping bags slowed them down. When they walked into the house, Shelly and Mrs. Foster were already in the front hall.

"You shouldn't have disappeared like that," Mrs. Foster scolded Shelly. "All your friends are upstairs."

"They're not my friends," Shelly replied in a grumpy voice. "They're your students."

Mrs. Foster noticed the Pony Pals. "Introduce yourselves to my daughter," she said. She turned to Shelly. "The tall one is taking the clinic."

"Hi," said Pam. "I'm Pam Crandal." She smiled at Shelly. "The tall one."

Shelly didn't smile back.

"I'm Lulu Sanders," said Lulu. She turned to Anna. "And this is Anna Harley. We saw a cute palomino pony in the field. What's her name?"

"Goldie," answered Shelly.

"Hi, Shelly," said Anna. "Lulu and I aren't taking the clinic, but we brought our ponies."

"So?" said Shelly.

Lulu thought Shelly was the rudest girl she'd ever met.

Anna thought that Shelly was very angry or very sad. Or both.

Pam was glad Shelly wasn't in the clinic.

"Shelly, bring Pam to your room," directed

Mrs. Foster. "She's sharing with you and Brooke. Anna and Lulu are in the guest room down here."

Anna and Lulu exchanged a glance.

"We thought that we'd be in the same room," Lulu told Mrs. Foster. "The three of us."

"Pam needs to be with the other clinic girls," Mrs. Foster told Anna and Lulu. "I'll bring you to your room. Then you can take care of your ponies."

Anna and Lulu picked up their suitcases and sleeping bags and followed Mrs. Foster down the hall. "Your two ponies will stay in one of the paddocks," she told them. She turned and looked at Lulu. "Your ponies are used to being outside, aren't they? Shelly will show you which paddock."

"They're always outside," answered Lulu.

"Pam's pony likes to be outside, too," added Anna.

"Pam's pony will be in the barn with the clinic horses," said Mrs. Foster.

Mrs. Foster opened the door to a small

bedroom and turned on the light. There were twin beds and a window facing the field and paddocks.

"You girls settle in," said Mrs. Foster. "Shelly will be down in a minute."

Meanwhile, Pam was following Shelly into a large bedroom on the third floor. The room had twin beds and a cot set up in a corner. A girl with long black hair sat on the edge of one of the beds filing her nails. Pam put her sleeping bag on the cot and her suitcase on the floor.

The girl on the bed looked up. "Hi," she said. "I'm Brooke."

Pam said hi back and introduced herself.

The phone by the bed rang and Shelly picked it up. "Yeah?" she said into the receiver. When she hung up the phone, Shelly turned to Pam. "That was my mother," she said. "I have to show your friends where to put your horses. You have a clinic meeting with my mother now. Tell Brooke."

Pam didn't bother to tell Shelly her horse

was a pony. Shelly had already left the room.

Pam turned to Brooke. "Shelly said to tell you that —"

Brooke rolled her eyes at Pam. "I heard her," she said. "I'm right here."

Pam felt embarrassed.

"There's something you should know," Brooke said as she stood up. "Shelly and I are fighting. We don't talk to each other anymore."

Pam was about to ask Brooke why they were fighting.

"Don't ask me about it," Brooke continued. "Really. It's between me and Shelly."

"Okay," Pam said as she followed Brooke out of the room. She wished with all her heart that Anna and Lulu were her roommates instead of Shelly and Brooke.

Lulu and Anna followed Shelly outside. Anna tried to get a conversation going. "We heard there are great trails around here," she said.

"Really?" said Shelly sarcastically as she

opened the gate to the field with the three ponies. "Which one is Pam's?" she asked.

"The chestnut one," answered Anna. "Her name is Lightning." Anna didn't mention the lucky upside-down heart marking on Lightning's forehead. She had a feeling Shelly wouldn't care.

"Okay, put your two ponies in the empty paddock next to the field," instructed Shelly. "After you feed them I'll show you where to put the other one." She put her headphones back on and faced the barn.

A half hour later the ponies were fed, and Lightning was settled in her stall. Anna and Lulu went back to the house with Shelly. They heard sounds of laughter coming from a room on the first floor.

"They're having a meeting," commented Shelly.

"Shouldn't we go?" asked Lulu.

"Are you in the clinic?" Shelly asked.

"No," answered Anna. "But we haven't met any of the other girls and —"

"Don't worry," said Shelly. "You're not missing anything."

"Do you want to play cards with us?" Anna asked. "We brought a deck of cards that are really neat. They have a picture of Black Beauty on them."

"I'm going to watch TV," said Shelly. She turned and went up the stairs without saying good night.

Sunday, 9:30 P.M.

Dear Journal,
   I am at Foster's Junior
Equitation and Jumping Clinic.
We had a meeting tonight.
Anna and Lulu weren't invited
to the first part. They were
taking care of our ponies.
   Anyway, at the meeting we
introduced ourselves. There
are five other girls in the
clinic. Brooke, Olivia, Jenny,
Maria, and Tonya. They all
know one another. I'm the
youngest and the only one
with a pony. We also had to
say what competitions we've
been in. I don't like to talk

37

about winning and who's the best. The other girls loved saying how many ribbons and trophies they won. They've been in so many competitions. They must go to a different one every weekend.

Anna and Lulu were invited for the second part of the meeting. Mrs. Foster introduced Anna and Lulu to everyone. She said they weren't in the clinic, but could watch and help with the jump set ups.

There are a lot of rules, like we're not allowed to leave our rooms after lights-out. We have to keep exactly to the schedule. There's even a bell to help us do everything on time.

When the meeting ended
we had to go straight to
our rooms. Lulu told me
that Lightning was in the
barn. Mrs. Foster wouldn't
let her stay out with
Acorn and Snow White.
That made me sad. We're
split up and our ponies
are, too.

I think Jenny is the
nicest of the other girls.
She asked me where I
was from. Brooke is definite-
ly the least nice person in
the clinic. She acts snobby.
After the meeting she smiled
her fake smile at Anna
and Lulu. "You girls still
have ponies," she said.
"How cute!" Brooke and I
share a room with Shelly
Foster. Brooke and Shelly

aren't talking to each other.
It's awful. I hate sharing
a room with them.

Brooke did say one
thing to Shelly before we
went to bed. She said,
" You've changed a lot.
Other people lose — "
Shelly shouted at Brooke
to shut up. She said, " I
told you I don't want to
talk about _that_. Ever! "
I wonder what _that_ is.
Did Shelly lose some
important competition?

I'm writing with a
flashlight under the
covers. I wish I hadn't
come to this clinic. It
was a big mistake. I
wish we could go home
right now. I hate it here.

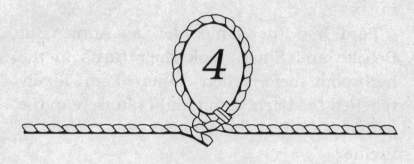

Secrets

The loud *dong-dong, dong-dong* of a bell woke Anna and Lulu the next morning. A minute later, Mrs. Foster knocked on their bedroom door. "Are you girls up?" she asked.

"Yes," answered Anna and Lulu in sleepy unison.

"See you all at the barn in thirty minutes," Mrs. Foster reminded them. "We have to keep to our schedule."

"Let's hurry, Lulu," said Anna as she jumped out of bed. "Maybe we can see Pam before everybody else gets there. I bet she'll hurry, too."

Pam had the same idea as Anna. But Brooke and Shelly took their turns in the bathroom before her. When Pam finally reached the barn, Anna and Lulu were in the paddock feeding their ponies. Pam waved to them.

"Pam, hurry up," Mrs. Foster yelled from the barn. "Everyone else is here."

I'll sit with Anna and Lulu at breakfast, thought Pam as she ran to the barn.

Anna and Lulu looked at the fields and hills beyond the Foster Farm.

"I bet there are some great trails in there," said Lulu.

"I bet Mrs. Foster won't even let us ride on them," said Anna. Anna noticed the palomino pony standing at the fence line. "Look," she whispered to Lulu.

The pony was watching Acorn and Snow White. Acorn looked up and saw him. The pony whinnied a friendly hello. The two ponies met at the fence and sniffed faces.

The bell rang again. Lulu looked at her watch. "It's seven-thirty," she said. "Time for breakfast."

"This bell thing is worse than being in school," said Anna. "I thought we were on vacation."

"Let's hurry so we can sit with Pam," suggested Lulu.

"It's so weird being here together and not being together," said Lulu as she followed Anna out of the paddock.

"Very weird," agreed Anna.

Lulu's stomach rumbled. She wondered what they'd have for breakfast.

A big table was set for them in the dining room. The food was lined up on a sideboard. A man dressed in a business suit was finishing his breakfast. He looked up and smiled at Anna and Lulu. "I'm Mr. Foster," he said.

Anna and Lulu introduced themselves.

"Nice to meet you," Mr. Foster said. "I'm off to work. Have a good day in your clinic."

He was gone before Lulu could tell him that they weren't in the clinic.

Pam filled her plate with bacon, scrambled eggs, and toast. As Anna and Lulu picked up their plates, Shelly came into the dining room. She looked grumpier and sadder than ever. What is her problem? wondered Anna.

"Pam, you sit between Jenny and Brooke at my end of the table," said Mrs. Foster.

"I was going to sit with Anna and Lulu," said Pam.

"You're part of the equestrian clinic this week," Mrs. Foster said sharply. "Not the Pony Pals."

Pam sat between Jenny and Brooke. Brooke turned to her. "The Pony Pals," she said in a teasing voice. "What's that all about?"

A couple of girls giggled.

"Quit it!" Shelly shouted at Brooke.

The room became silent.

"Please, Shelly," said Mrs. Foster. "Just serve yourself breakfast and sit down."

Shelly made herself a bowl of cereal, and everyone else went back to eating and talking.

Shelly sat next to Anna. "Don't pay any attention to Brooke," she said softly. "She's just mad at me." Shelly put on her Walkman headphones and listened to music while she finished her breakfast. Anna was disappointed. She wanted to talk to Shelly Foster. She was very curious about her.

After breakfast, everyone but Shelly went to the riding ring. Mrs. Foster told Anna and Lulu to sit on two chairs near the door. "I don't need your help with this first lesson," she told them, "so you can just watch."

The riders walked, trotted, and cantered. Next, they practiced figure eights and serpentines.

"Pam's as good as any of them," Anna whispered to Lulu.

"I bet she's as good at jumping, too," said Lulu.

"Quiet, you two," Mrs. Foster ordered. "Watch carefully. You can learn a lot just by observing."

"I can learn how to be bored," mumbled Anna.

After the morning lesson, everyone went to the barn for the horse-care class. Mrs. Foster's barn assistant, Tilden, showed them the best way to groom a horse. They practiced on their own horses and ponies.

The afternoon jumping class was in the outside ring. Anna and Lulu moved the jumps. Anna thought Pam was as good as any of the other riders at jumping. Except maybe Brooke.

After the class, Mrs. Foster asked Anna and Lulu to put the jumps away.

"I'll help them," offered Pam.

Lulu and Anna exchanged a glance. This would be their chance to finally talk to Pam.

"You can't help them, Pam," said Mrs. Foster. "You have to cool down Lightning and settle her in the barn."

Pam and the other riders left the ring.

"I'm going to ask Mrs. Foster if we can go for a trail ride," Anna told Lulu. "And if Pam can come."

"She'll just say no," Lulu warned.

Anna ran after Mrs. Foster. A minute later she was back in the ring.

"You were right," she told Lulu. "Mrs. Foster said we can't go trail riding without a guide. And Pam can't go during clinic week."

"Why?" asked Lulu.

Anna put her hands on her hips and imitated Mrs. Foster. "The clinic riders and their mounts need all their energy for the clinic," she said in a stern voice.

Lulu laughed at Anna's imitation of Mrs. Foster.

Anna went back to talking like herself. "I'm fed up," she said.

"We have a Pony Pal Problem," said Lulu, "and we can't even talk to Pam about it."

"This whole place is a Pony Pal Problem for us," said Anna.

"Let's write Pam a note," suggested Lulu. "We'll set up a meeting after everyone is asleep. It's the only time."

"We aren't supposed to leave our rooms after the last bell," Anna reminded Lulu. "Pam doesn't like to break rules."

"This is an emergency," said Lulu.

After Anna and Lulu put away the jumps, they went to their room. Lulu wrote the note and Anna drew a picture on it.

Pam —
   We need to have an emergency Pony Pal meeting. Here's what we should talk about:
1. How can the three of us be together here?

2. What is Shelly's problem? Why is she so sad and angry all the time?
3. What are Shelly and Brooke fighting about?

Meet us tonight after
everyone goes to sleep.
Come to our room.
P. S. Your riding and
jumping are excellent
in the clinic.

At dinner, Lulu stood behind Pam in the food line. She stuck the folded note in Pam's back jeans pocket. "Pony Pal message in your pocket," she whispered in Pam's ear.

Brooke came up behind Lulu and tapped her on the shoulder. "Do the little Pony Pals have secrets?" she asked.

Lulu swung around and faced her. "Leave us alone, Brooke," she hissed.

"Oh, *puh-lease*," sighed Brooke. "I don't even know what you two are doing here."

Neither do I, thought Lulu.

During dinner, Pam excused herself to go to the bathroom. She read the note from Anna and Lulu. When she came back to the table, she smiled and nodded to her friends. She couldn't wait to be alone with them. She had something important to tell them about Shelly Foster.

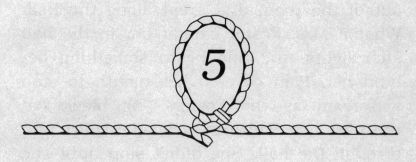

Alarm

Anna and Lulu changed into their pajamas and played cards while they waited for Pam.

They were still waiting for her at ten-thirty.

"Maybe Shelly and Brooke stayed awake reading," suggested Lulu.

"Or arguing," said Anna.

Lulu was right. Shelly read in bed for a long time before turning out her light. Pam listened as Shelly's breathing slowed down and little snoring noises came from Brooke's bed. Pam checked her watch. 10:31.

Pam's heart pounded as she sneaked out of the room and crept along the hall. What if Mrs. Foster caught her in the hall after lights-out? She heard something behind her. Pam covered her mouth to stop a scream as the Fosters' big black cat ran past her. Pam ran down the stairs and through the hall. She didn't stop until she was in Anna and Lulu's room. She closed the door behind her.

The three friends met in a big hug.

"Did anyone see you?" asked Anna.

"Just the cat," answered Pam.

Tears sprang to Pam's eyes.

"What's wrong?" asked Anna.

"I'm sorry I brought you here," said Pam. "I'm so sorry."

Lulu patted her arm. "Don't feel bad, Pam," she said.

"It's not your fault," added Anna. "We wanted to come. Remember?"

"Our room is nice," said Lulu.

Anna pointed to the window. "And we can see Snow White and Acorn from here."

The three girls went to the window and looked out at the moonlit paddock.

"Where?" asked Pam. "I don't see them."

Lulu looked over the paddock. She didn't see the ponies, either. "They're not there," she said in an alarmed voice.

"Maybe Mrs. Foster put them in the barn," suggested Pam.

"I just saw them in there a little while ago," said Anna.

Lulu's heart beat faster. What if Snow White had run away again? What if she was frightened or injured?

"Quick," said Anna. "Get dressed. We have to go find them."

Lulu lent Pam a pair of jeans, sneakers, and a sweater.

The Pony Pals dressed quickly.

"Bring your flashlight, Lulu," said Pam.

Lulu pulled her flashlight out of her backpack. "We'll use it to look for their tracks," she said.

"We should pick up their lead ropes from the tack room," said Anna.

"And the first aid kit," said Lulu. "Just in case."

The three girls ran quietly down the dark hall. They were at the front door when someone came up behind them. "What are you three up to?" a voice asked.

The Pony Pals turned to face Shelly Foster.

Anna put her fingers to her lips. "Shh," she warned Shelly.

"Our ponies are missing," said Lulu in a hushed voice. "Snow White and Acorn aren't in the paddock."

"Please help us," whispered Pam.

Shelly stared at them. Anna couldn't tell if she was going to tell on them or help them.

"I'm so afraid Snow White will get hurt," said Lulu. "She's had lots of accidents."

"Shelly, will you help us find them?" asked Pam. "You know your way around here."

Shelly finally spoke. "Don't worry," she said. "We'll find them."

"Thank you," said Lulu.

"I'll get dressed and meet you at the barn," whispered Shelly.

"We'll get their lead ropes," said Pam as she unlocked and opened the front door.

"Don't do that!" Shelly exclaimed. But it was too late. The shriek of a burglar alarm screamed through the house.

In an instant, Mr. and Mrs. Foster were in the hall and girls were running down the stairs. Everyone was in nightclothes except the Pony Pals.

"What is going on here?" shouted Mrs. Foster. "Where do you think you are going?"

"Our ponies aren't in the paddock," Lulu told Mrs. and Mr. Foster.

"We looked for them out the bedroom window and they're not there," said Anna.

"We have to find them," added Pam.

"They've escaped, then," said Mrs. Foster. "How troublesome."

Lulu noticed that Mr. Foster went into the office.

"Those ponies don't know their way around here," said Shelly. "They could get hurt or really lost."

"Ponies are strong," Mrs. Foster told her.

"And smart. Certainly, you know that, Shelly."

"Please let us go look for our ponies," begged Lulu. "We have to."

"I'll help you," said Jenny.

"Me, too," said Olivia.

Mr. Foster came to the door of the office. "Come in here, girls," he said. "I've found your ponies."

"Our ponies are in the office?!" exclaimed Anna as she rushed in. She looked around the room. No ponies.

Mr. Foster pointed to the video monitor for the security system. On the screen Anna saw the back end of a white pony and half of Acorn's face. Lightning's head was hanging out the window of her stall.

"Snow White and Acorn went to find Lightning," said Anna excitedly. "They missed her."

"She must have missed them, too," said Pam.

Snow White is safe, thought Lulu. She's safe.

The other girls were looking at the ponies

on the TV screen and talking about how cute they were.

"They love to be together," said Lulu.

"They're best friends," added Anna as she exchanged a smile with Pam.

"Shetlands are smart, stubborn little fellows, aren't they?" said Mr. Foster.

"They sure are," agreed Anna. "Acorn knows lots of tricks, too."

"I used to have a pony," said Jenny. "We sold her when I got Gilder. I love Gilder but I still miss my pony."

Shelly suddenly turned and ran out of the office.

"Shelly," called Mrs. Foster.

"Leave me alone!" Shelly shouted at her mother.

Mr. Foster walked to the office door. "I'll talk to her," he said sadly.

"Mrs. Foster, we'll go get our ponies," said Anna quietly.

Mrs. Foster turned to her. "They'll just escape again," she said. "We need to put them in the barn."

"They'll stay in the paddock if Lightning is with them," said Lulu.

"Please let Lightning stay with Acorn and Snow White," pleaded Pam. "Lightning doesn't like being in a barn that much, anyway."

Mrs. Foster looked around at the Pony Pals and sighed. "Okay," she said. "But then the three of you go to bed."

Anna was already at the front door. When she opened it the alarm went off again. Everyone laughed. Everyone but Mrs. Foster. She just looked sad.

LULU'S JOURNAL

Travel Journal.
Foster Farm, Virginia.
        Tuesday morning.
                6:30 A.M.

Last night, Snow
white and Acorn
jumped the fence and
went to find Lightning.
More about that later.
Anyway, Mrs. Foster
let us put our three
ponies together in the
paddock. We watched
them running in the
moonlight. They were
so happy to be together
again. We were, too.
    Pam found out
something about
Shelly Foster. There
are a lot of framed

riding pictures in the third-floor hall. Pam was looking at them. One was of Shelly on a black pony. Jenny came up beside Pam. She told Pam that the pony's name was Midnight Ride and that he died two months ago. Mrs. Foster told the girls not to talk about it, because Shelly is so upset. But everybody knows. Now we know, too. Shelly is sad because her pony died.

Pam thinks that Shelly acts more angry than sad. Anna said sometimes when people are sad they're a little angry. Shelly is a *lot* angry at her mother. We all wonder why.

Pam and I don't like Shelly very much. Anna said we should still help her. We all agreed that Shelly should be our Pony Pal project while we're here.

Pam said Shelly is more a Pony Pal Problem than a project.

We're going to have a Pony Pal meeting in the paddock after the morning lesson today. We'll each have an idea of how to help Shelly. I have four hours to come up with an idea.

I hope I can. There's the morning bell. Time to get dressed and feed the ponies. L.S.

P.S. Mrs. Foster knocked on our door and said she wants to see Pam, Anna, and me in the office before breakfast. I bet we're in trouble for what happened last night. More later. L.S.

Three Ideas

Anna and Lulu quickly dressed and ran out to the field. Pam was there feeding their ponies. Lulu told Pam that Mrs. Foster wanted to see them before breakfast.

"What do you think she wants?" asked Lulu.

"I think she's mad at us," said Anna, "because of last night."

"Maybe she'll send us home," said Pam.

"I don't want to go home," said Anna. "I want to stay and help Shelly."

"Me, too," added Lulu.

A few minutes later the Pony Pals were in Mrs. Foster's office. She was printing out the day's riding lesson. She looked up at the girls. "Anna and Lulu, you can take the morning flat-work class," she said. "We'll make room for you in the ring. Now go along to breakfast."

The Pony Pals looked at one another in amazement. Mrs. Foster didn't scold them. She was actually being nice to them.

Pam was happy that her friends would be in the class.

Anna was glad that Acorn would get to show off a little.

Lulu thought that taking a class would be more interesting than watching one.

As the Pony Pals were going in to breakfast, Shelly was walking out.

"Hi," said Anna and Lulu in unison.

Shelly ignored them and kept walking.

"It's going to be hard to help Shelly," Pam whispered to Anna. "She's so rude to us."

"But we can't give up on her," Anna whispered back.

"I keep thinking about how I'd feel if Snow White died," added Lulu in a hushed voice. "We *have* to help Shelly."

Brooke pushed past them. "More Pony Pal secrets?" she asked in a sarcastic voice.

"Yes," said Lulu. "And they're all about you, Brooke."

Anna and Pam laughed.

"Babies," mumbled Brooke.

After breakfast, Anna and Lulu saddled up their ponies and joined the flat-work class. They smiled at each other across the ring. It felt good to be riding instead of watching.

After the lesson, the three friends led the ponies back to the field. While they took off the tack and cooled down the ponies, they had their Pony Pal meeting.

Pam began. "I didn't write down my idea," she said. "It's not really an idea about what to do. It's something Jenny told me about Shelly."

"What?" asked Lulu.

"She's angry at her mother and Brooke because of Midnight Ride," answered Pam.

"What about Midnight Ride?" asked Anna.

"It happened last year, at this clinic," explained Pam. "Mrs. Foster kept nagging Shelly in front of the other girls. She wanted her to trade Midnight Ride for a good jumping horse. Brooke wanted Shelly to give up her pony, too. She told Shelly it was silly to have a pony when you could have a big horse. Shelly didn't want to give up Midnight Ride. Besides, she was sick of jumping and going to all these competitions with her mother. She wanted to have a backyard pony and go for trail rides — like us. Midnight Ride was perfect for that."

"Her mother wanted her to give up her pony," said Anna sadly.

"And then her pony died," added Lulu.

"I bet she thinks her mother is glad that Midnight Ride died," said Anna.

"That's exactly what she thinks," concluded Pam.

"That's awful," said Anna.

"No wonder she's angry," added Lulu.

The three friends were silent as they rubbed down their ponies. They were all thinking about how Shelly must feel.

Pam rubbed the heart marking on Lightning's forehead. We need good luck to help Shelly, she thought.

Lulu broke the silence. "What's your idea, Anna?" she asked.

Anna opened her sketchbook and handed it to Lulu. Lulu and Pam looked at the drawing.

"Shelly should talk about her pony," explained Anna. "She's keeping everything inside. When someone dies, it's good to talk about it."

"You're right, Anna," agreed Pam. "But how do we get Shelly to talk about Midnight Ride? She won't talk to us about *anything*."

"My idea might help with that," said Lulu.

She handed a slip of paper to Pam. Pam read Lulu's idea out loud.

Write a letter to Shelly.
Tell her we want to
be her friends and
invite her on a trail ride.

"Jenny told me that Shelly loves to go trail riding," said Pam.

"Maybe she'll ride Goldie, the palomino pony," suggested Anna. "She's a nice pony."

"Shh," cautioned Pam. "Here comes Olivia."

"Pam," called Olivia, "there's a lesson on

cleaning tack. Hurry up. Anna and Lulu should come, too."

"When can we write the letter to Shelly?" asked Anna.

"This afternoon at snack time," answered Pam. "We'll meet in your room."

The girls hurried toward the barn.

A few hours later the Pony Pals sat on the bed in Anna and Lulu's room and wrote the letter.

Dear Shelly,
    We know why you feel sad. We are very sorry that your pony died. Our friend's pony, Winston, died. We honored him in a parade It is sad when a pony dies.
    Do you want to go for a trail ride with us? It would be a good way to remember your happy times with Midnight Ride.

Please tell us if you want
to be our friend.
The Pony Pals,
Pam, Anna, Lulu
P.S. Anna and Lulu are not
going to watch the video
tonight. They're going to
hang out in their room.
You're invited.

Pam carefully folded the letter and put it in her pocket. "I'll give it to Shelly," she said. "She's usually in her room before dinner."

"I hope she reads it," said Lulu.

"I hope she likes it, and that she'll talk to us," added Anna.

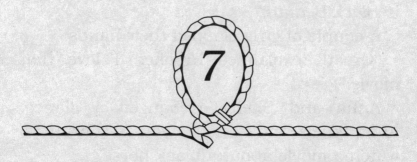

Sodas and Chips

Shelly was late for dinner that night. Anna thought she looked sadder than ever. When Shelly sat down next to her, Anna smiled and said hello.

Shelly leaned toward Anna. "I'll come to your room tonight," she whispered. "But I don't want to talk about Midnight. Okay?"

"Okay," Anna whispered back. "I'm glad you're coming."

Shelly didn't say anything else to Anna.

During dessert, Mrs. Foster tapped her glass for attention. The room went silent. "Everyone," she announced, "the video tonight is *Black Beauty.*"

A couple of girls clapped their hands.

"Great!" exclaimed Brooke. "I love that movie."

Anna and Shelly exchanged a glance. Anna knew that Shelly wouldn't want to watch a movie about a black horse.

"I already saw it," Anna whispered in Shelly's ear. "Lulu, too. We're not going."

"Me, neither," said Shelly.

After dinner, Anna and Lulu went to their room. While they were waiting for Shelly, Lulu wrote in her journal. Anna sat at the window and drew the view. A half hour passed. Finally, there was a knock on the door.

Anna looked up from her drawing. "Come in," she called.

Shelly walked in carrying a bag. She held it up. "I brought us some sodas and chips," she said, smiling.

Lulu and Anna thanked Shelly and they each took a soda. Shelly noticed Anna's drawing. "Can I look at it?" she asked.

"Sure," said Anna.

"She draws great," said Lulu.

Shelly sat next to Anna and looked at all of the drawings in her book.

"These are good," said Shelly. "You're a very good artist."

Anna smiled a thank-you.

Lulu pulled a chair up next to Shelly and Anna at the window. The three girls watched the sunset while they talked.

At first, Shelly asked Anna and Lulu questions about Wiggins and their lives there. They told her some of their Pony Pal adventures.

"Tell me about the pony you knew that died," said Shelly. "What did he die from?"

Anna and Lulu told Shelly all about Winston and his owner, Ms. Wiggins.

"Winston died of old age," explained Lulu. "He was thirty years old. We stayed with him all night long before he died."

"We took turns watching," added Anna. "Acorn and Winston were special friends."

"After he died, Ms. Wiggins showed us lots

of old pictures of him," said Lulu. "We all cried. We were so sad."

The three girls were silent.

"I was the only one who cried when Midnight Ride died," whispered Shelly.

Anna looked over at her. Shelly's eyes were filled with tears.

"I'm sorry," said Anna.

Lulu put her arm around Shelly's shoulder. "Me, too," she said.

"Do you want to talk about him?" asked Anna.

"I can't," said Shelly. "It'd be too sad."

"We don't mind if you're sad," said Lulu.

"Tell us about the day you got him," suggested Anna.

The girls sat in the dark and Shelly told them the story of her pony. Some parts of the story were funny, and they laughed. But by the time she finished, they were all crying.

"Those are wonderful stories," said Lulu as she handed Shelly a tissue. "I think you should write them all down."

"You could put them in a book," added Anna, "with photos."

"That will just make me sadder," said Shelly.

"It will make you happy, too," said Lulu. "Your pony was so funny. It will help keep his memory alive."

"A memory book," said Shelly thoughtfully. "If I do it, will you draw some pictures for it, Anna?"

"Sure," agreed Anna. "Let's start tomorrow."

"Will you go on a trail ride with us, too?" asked Lulu. "We don't know where to go."

"I don't want to ride anymore," said Shelly.

"Midnight Ride wouldn't want you to stop riding," said Anna.

"You're right," agreed Shelly. "But if I ride my mother will want me to jump again. She'll want me to get a horse and be in competitions."

"Just because you go on a trail ride with us?" said Lulu.

"My mom wants me to be a big-deal rider

more than anything," said Shelly. "And I don't want that. I never did." Tears came into Shelly's eyes again. Her voice lowered to a whisper. "I think she was glad when Midnight Ride died. She thought I'd finally get a good jumping horse."

"You have a big problem with your mother," said Anna.

Suddenly, the overhead light went on. "What are you all doing in the dark?" asked Pam.

"Talking," said the three girls in unison. They looked at one another in the bright light and smiled.

The bell rang for bedtime. Shelly stood up. "I'm going upstairs," she said. "I have something I want to write." She smiled at Pam. "Come on, Pam. I'll tell you all about it."

After Pam and Shelly left, Anna and Lulu put on their pajamas and turned out the light. They lay in the dark talking about Shelly and her mother.

"I wish we could help them," said Lulu, "but I don't know how."

Words and Pictures

The next morning, Shelly sat next to Anna at breakfast again. "I worked on the memory book last night," Shelly said. "While you take your lesson this morning, I'm going to find some photos for it."

"That's great!" said Anna. "I'll draw for you this afternoon. Can Lulu help with the book, too?"

"Okay," agreed Shelly. "She can paste in the photos."

That afternoon the three girls sat in Anna and Lulu's bedroom and worked on the memory book. After her jumping lesson, Pam joined them. By dinnertime, the book was finished.

Shelly looked around at her new friends. "Thank you for helping me," she said. "I wish I could do something for you."

"You can," said Anna. "Take us on a trail ride."

"We thought Anna and Lulu would be able to trail ride every day," explained Pam. "But your mother won't let them go without a guide."

Shelly looked at the Pony Pals thoughtfully. "I want to take you," she said. "But I can't. If I ride, my mother will start nagging me again about competing."

"I have an idea," said Anna as she stood up. "We'll ask her together. Your mother won't nag you if we're there."

"My mother can be stubborn," said Shelly.

Pam put her hands on her hips. "If she gives you a hard time," she said, "we'll take your side. You should ride again if you're ready to."

Shelly closed her memory book and stood up. "Okay," she agreed. "Let's go find my mom before dinner."

Anna, Pam, and Shelly headed out of the room.

Lulu noticed that Shelly had left her memory book. It gave Lulu an idea. She picked up the book and followed the others.

The girls found Mrs. Foster in her office.

"Hello, girls," she said. "You did some pretty fabulous jumping today, Pam. You'll win lots of competitions. Your mother and Eleanor Morgan will be proud of you."

"My mother doesn't care that much about competitions," said Pam. "She just wants Lightning and me to enjoy riding."

"Surely you compete," said Mrs. Foster. "You go to shows?"

"My mother takes her students to a lot of shows," explained Pam. "But I don't always go."

"You should go to *all* the competitions," Mrs. Foster said. "They're fun."

"Not for me," mumbled Shelly.

"Some people like horse shows more than others, Mrs. Foster," Anna explained. "I like trail riding the best."

"Me, too," said Pam and Lulu in unison.

"We wondered if we could go on a trail ride tomorrow," added Anna.

"I already told you, no trail riding without a guide," said Mrs. Foster crossly. "Someone has to go with you."

"I'll take them," said Shelly softly.

"And ride?" said Mrs. Foster with surprise.

"Yes," answered Shelly. "I'll take Goldie."

"Why don't you take my horse?" said Mrs. Foster excitedly. "You really are ready for her, darling. Royal Star is such a sweet jumper. You could join the clinic classes with him."

"I don't want to ride your horse!" Shelly cried. "I don't want to take the clinic. I don't want to go to another horse show for as long as I live." Angry tears were streaming down Shelly's face. She ran from the room.

Mrs. Foster jumped up to follow her.

"Leave me alone!" Shelly shouted over her shoulder.

Mrs. Foster stopped in the doorway and tears welled up in her eyes.

"Shelly thinks that you're glad Midnight Ride died," Lulu said softly.

Mrs. Foster turned toward her. "What?" she said, horrified. "How could she think such a terrible thing?"

"Because you wanted her to give him up," explained Pam. "And she didn't want to."

"She misses her pony," said Anna. "She wrote this book about him."

Lulu handed Mrs. Foster the memory book.

The Pony Pals left to find Shelly.

Mrs. Foster opened the memory book and read it.

midnight Ride

by Shelly Foster

Anna

When I was a little girl my mother gave me lessons on the school pony, Goldie. Other kids took lessons on Goldie, too. So I didn't feel like Goldie was MY pony. I begged my parents for a pony of my own.

On the morning of my sixth birthday, my mother woke me up as usual. I got dressed and went downstairs. I was happy because it was my birthday and I was going to have a party in the afternoon. I was thinking about the party when I went into the kitchen. That's the first time I saw Midnight Ride. He was standing in the kitchen with a big red bow around his neck. I couldn't believe my eyes!

Midnight Ride and I were best friends right away. I loved the sparkle in his eyes. I loved to rub my hands on his fur. He had the silkiest coat!

Midnight Ride and
Goldie became stablemates.
They were both very playful
and always getting into
trouble. Here are some of
the funny things they did.

I went on a trail ride with my mom and some of her students. We played Frisbee before lunch. That's when Midnight Ride and Goldie ate half our sandwiches!

Jenny and I used to sneak Midnight Ride into the kitchen when my mom wasn't around. Midnight Ride loved the kitchen. It was fun. We'd give him a carrot or an apple and all have our snack together.

One day, midnight Ride
escaped and followed the
school bus. Of course, Goldie
followed him.

Jenny and Olivia had ponies,
too. We played with our
ponies all the time. Sometimes
we dressed them up.

My pony loved to go on trail rides. He was interested in everything around him. He would stop and watch a squirrel in a tree. He hardly ever got spooked. But we didn't have much time for trail rides. My mother took me to all the riding competitions. Midnight Ride only came if we were competing. When we were in competitions we usually won a ribbon. But we weren't always in first place. That would disappoint my mother.

I was proud of Midnight Ride, anyway. We didn't like going to competitions very much. We also didn't like taking jumping lessons. We both liked trail rides much, much better.

Midnight Ride was only five years old when I got him. I thought I would have him a long, long time. But now he is gone. He died in the summertime. Here is what happened. First, he didn't want to eat. We called the vet. Midnight Ride had colic. The next day he died from it.

When Midnight Ride died I lost my best friend. No one understands how sad and lonely I am. Some people don't keep their ponies for a long time. They have a pony and then they get a horse. That's okay for them. But I wanted to keep Midnight Ride forever. Now he's gone. All I have left are memories.

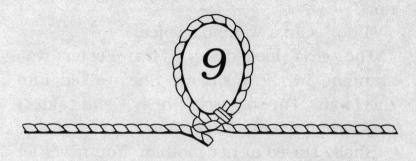

Late for Dinner

The Pony Pals looked for Shelly in her room, in the yard, and in the barn. They finally found her in Anna and Lulu's room. She was sitting on Anna's bed, crying.

"I don't want to live here anymore," she sobbed. "I'm going to run away."

Anna sat next to Shelly and put her arm around her shoulder. "You can come to Wiggins with us if you want," said Anna. "But don't run away."

"You should give your mother another

chance," said Pam. "Maybe she understands now."

"I do," said a woman's voice.

The girls looked up. Mrs. Foster was standing in the doorway. She walked into the room. "I'm so sorry, Shelly," she said. "I was wrong. Please forgive me."

Shelly stared at her mother. "You never let me do what I want," she said in a low voice. "I always have to do what you want."

"I was wrong," said Mrs. Foster. "Please, Shelly, don't give up riding because of me. You don't have to go to competitions if you don't want to. Ride Goldie. She can be your pony now. And please, please try to forgive me."

Shelly didn't say anything. The room was silent.

Mrs. Foster sat on the bed next to Shelly. "I was never, ever glad that your lovely pony died," she said.

"You wanted me to trade him for a horse," said Shelly. "That's all you ever talked about."

"But I didn't want your pony to die, Shelly," repeated Mrs. Foster. "We all loved him." She put the memory book on Shelly's lap. "This book is so beautiful. It helped me remember him."

"I miss my pony," Shelly sobbed.

"I know, honey," said Mrs. Foster. "I should have been more understanding. I made a big mistake. I'm sorry."

Mrs. Foster put an arm around her daughter's shoulder. She was crying, too. Shelly leaned against her mother.

The Pony Pals quietly left the room. In the hall they hit silent high fives.

"Where's my family?" a man's voice boomed. Mr. Foster was walking toward them. "Where's the Missus? Where is Shelly?"

Pam told Mr. Foster that Shelly and her mother were in the guest room.

"Go to dinner, girls," he said. "The other girls are wondering where you've all gone to."

When the Pony Pals walked into the dining room, everyone looked up from their desserts.

"Where's Mrs. Foster?" asked Brooke.

"And Shelly?" added Olivia.

"Is everything okay?" asked Jenny.

"Everything's fine," answered Pam. She looked over at the food on the buffet. There was baked chicken, mashed potatoes, and a fancy-looking salad. It all looked delicious.

"But where are they?" insisted Brooke. "You know and you're not telling us. You have to tell."

Anna picked up her plate. "No we don't," she said.

Mrs. Foster walked into the dining room. "Shelly and I were having a private talk, Brooke," she said, "about Midnight Ride."

"Oh," said Brooke. "Does that mean we can talk about him, too?"

"Yes, you can," answered Mrs. Foster. "And I encourage you to do so."

A few minutes later, Shelly came into the dining room. Jenny jumped up and ran over to her. She hugged Shelly and said she was sorry that Midnight Ride had died. Olivia did the same thing.

Mrs. Foster tapped a glass for attention. "There will be no meeting tonight," she announced. "Tomorrow is the last day of the clinic. I want to congratulate you all. You've worked hard and well. I hope I haven't stressed competition too much with you. I want you to enjoy your riding, too."

Everyone clapped, including Shelly.

After dinner, Shelly and the Pony Pals went outside. Shelly ran over to the paddock Goldie shared with the four horses. When Goldie saw Shelly come through the gate, she trotted over to her. Shelly put her arms around the golden pony's neck. "You must miss Midnight Ride, too," she said.

Goldie nickered as if to say, "I do."

The Pony Pals watched from their ponies' paddock. "Let's put Goldie with our ponies," said Lulu.

Anna ran up to the fence to tell Shelly their idea.

"Goldie is such a sweet pony," said Shelly. "I bet she'd like to be with your ponies."

Soon the four ponies were in the paddock together. Goldie followed Acorn wherever he went.

"We can go on a trail ride tomorrow," Shelly told the Pony Pals. "My mother said Pam can come, too. We can take our lunch and have a picnic."

"That'll be so much fun," said Pam.

"It's like we'll all be Pony Pals," said Shelly. "Is that okay?"

"Of course it's okay," said Lulu.

"You *are* a Pony Pal," added Anna.

The girls hit high fives and shouted, "All right!"

Lightning joined in with a loud whinny. The four Pony Pals laughed.

Broken Wheel Farm

After breakfast the next morning, the four girls mounted their ponies.

"You go first, Shelly," suggested Pam. "You're our guide."

The trail went through woods and fields and around a mountain. It was beautiful and different from the woods around Wiggins.

After riding for two hours, Shelly showed her new friends her favorite spot for a picnic. It was beside a brook.

"Our favorite picnic spot in Wiggins is by a brook, too," Lulu told Shelly.

The four ponies drank from the brook and rested while the girls ate their lunch.

"Is this what the Pony Pals do all the time?" Shelly asked as she handed Anna a sandwich.

"Not ALL the time," answered Anna. "But we trail ride a lot."

"That's what I want to do," said Shelly. "Trail ride a lot."

"You need some friends to do it with, though," said Pam.

"You live too far away to ride with us," added Anna sadly.

"There are a lot of horse people around here," commented Lulu. "Some of them must like trail riding."

Shelly ate her sandwich and thought. "I know who I could ride with," she said finally. "The kids who hang out at Broken Wheel Farm. They used to ask me to ride with them. But I never had time because of the horse shows."

"Now you don't have to go to horse shows," said Pam as she stood up.

Shelly smiled. "I like those kids at Broken

Wheel," she said. "The farm is on our road. I could ride there."

"Perfect," said Anna.

It was time to head back. Anna and Lulu packed up the lunch things. Shelly and Pam prepared the ponies.

"Do we go back the same way we came?" Anna asked as she mounted Acorn.

"There is another way," explained Shelly. "But it's longer." She grinned at the Pony Pals. "Should we do it?"

"All right!" said the Pony Pals in unison.

The four girls had a wonderful time riding together. Anna thought it was one of the best trail rides of her life.

When they arrived back at the Foster Farm, Mrs. Crandal was driving up the driveway. It was time for the Pony Pals to go back to Wiggins.

"Do you have to go home so soon?" Shelly asked as she dismounted. "Can you stay over another night?"

"We have to go today," Pam explained. "My mother teaches tomorrow."

The Pony Pals and Shelly greeted Mrs. Crandal. Mrs. Foster praised Pam's work in the classes. "But I let her cut this last day," she explained. "She wanted to trail ride with Shelly, Anna, and Lulu."

"I'm glad she went with them," said Mrs. Crandal as she hugged her daughter. "She loves to trail ride with her friends."

"So does Shelly," said Mrs. Foster. Mrs. Foster smiled at her daughter. Shelly smiled back.

A half hour later, the ponies were in the horse trailer and the girls' suitcases and the tack trunks were packed. It was time to say good-bye.

The Pony Pals hugged Shelly.

"Thank you for getting me to make a memory book," Shelly whispered to them. "And for helping me with my mother. She understands me better now."

"I hope you girls will all come back," said Mrs. Foster. "The Pony Pals and their ponies are always welcome at Foster Farm."

Pam put a hand on Shelly's shoulder. "You

have a Pony Pal right here, Mrs. Foster," she said.

"Time to go, girls," said Mrs. Crandal. "We have a long drive ahead of us."

The girls said good-bye to Shelly and Mrs. Foster and climbed into the truck. Mrs. Crandal started the engine and they drove away from Foster Farm.

The Pony Pals waved to Shelly from the windows. "Write to us, Pony Pal," shouted Pam.

The drive back to Wiggins went by quickly. The girls told Mrs. Crandal all about their week. "You should have called me, Pam," said Mrs. Crandal. "I would have spoken to Mrs. Foster about the ponies and the sleeping arrangements for you girls. It was silly to split you three up."

"We wanted to solve the problems ourselves," said Lulu.

"And you did," said Mrs. Crandal. She smiled at the girls. "I'm so proud of all of you."

Four hours later, the pickup and horse trailer drove into Wiggins.

"We're back!" Anna yelled out the window.

An elderly couple walking around the town green waved to her. "Welcome home," they shouted.

The first stop was at Anna's house. Anna and Lulu led their ponies out of the trailer. "You were great," Lulu told Snow White. "I know I can take you in a trailer. You'll be a great traveler like Dad and me."

Grandmother Sanders hurried across the lawn toward them. She gave Lulu a big kiss and ran her hand along Snow White's neck. "I missed you, too, Snow White."

Mr. Harley came out and helped Anna and Lulu with their suitcases and pony supplies. Pam and Mrs. Crandal said good-bye to Anna and Lulu and drove home.

Dr. Crandal was waiting outside to greet them. He wrapped Pam in a big hug. "I missed you," he said. "Did you have a good time?"

"We had a wonderful time," answered Pam.

That night Pam lay in bed thinking about

the week in Virginia. She did have a wonderful time. Taking the classes was fun and interesting. In her head, she reviewed all that she learned. She wondered if she'd ever go to another clinic. I wouldn't want to go without my Pony Pals, she thought. Next she thought about Shelly. It was great to have a new Pony Pal, even if she did live far away.

Lulu kissed her grandmother good night and went up to her room. She was glad she had taken a lot of photos on the trip. I'll have them developed first thing tomorrow, she thought. It was my first trip with Snow White and my Pony Pals. I want to remember this trip always. I'll have copies of the photos made for Shelly, too, she decided. We'll send them to her when we write her a letter.

Anna looked out the window at Acorn in the paddock. He was sleeping near the shed. She liked how he made friends with Goldie, too. Anna smiled to herself. Acorn went looking for Lightning. Snow White went with him. Our ponies stick together, she thought. Just like the Pony Pals. Anna was proud of her pony. Anna wished that Shelly lived closer. She hoped that Shelly would make good friends at Broken Wheel Ranch.

Before Anna fell asleep she made a promise to herself. The next day the Pony Pals would write a letter to Shelly Foster, the fourth Pony Pal.

Dear Pam, Anna, and Lulu,

Thank you for the letter. I was so happy to receive it. The pictures Lulu took are great. I showed them to my new riding friends at Broken Wheel. The day after you left, I rode Goldie over there. I recognized one girl right away. Her name is Mary Ellen. Her parents own Broken Wheel. Mary Ellen's pony is a Welsh pony, like Snow White, only brown. His name is Runabout. It's a good name for him, because he's always running in the field. Mary Ellen said she saw me in a horse show with Midnight Ride. She wondered why I wasn't riding him. I told her that Midnight Ride died. The next day she came to my house, and I showed her the memory book.

Goldie is so sweet and a great ride. She loves being on trails as much as Midnight Ride. Here's the biggest news: I can ride Goldie over to Broken Wheel Farm after school and on weekends. My mom doesn't mind. Another girl I met at Broken Wheel is Linda. Linda has a brown-and-white Appaloosa named Smoothie. And guess what? Smoothie has a smooth gait. Mary Ellen and Linda have been best friends for a long time. I wondered if I could be friends with both of them, too. Guess what? All three of us are best friends now. You would love Mary Ellen and Linda. If we lived in Wiggins or you lived near us, there would be SIX Pony Pals.

Tonight we are having our first barn sleep over. Tomorrow we're

going on the trail ride I took
with you. We call ourselves Pony
Pals, too. I hope you don't mind.

When Midnight Ride died I
thought I would never be happy
again. I still miss my pony, but
I am happy. Happy to ride. Happy
to be with my new friends. Happy
to be a Pony Pal.

Write again soon and tell me
about your Pony Pal adventures.
Linda, Mary Ellen, and I will write
back and tell you about ours.

                Your Pony Pal from Virginia,
                    Shelly and Goldie

Dear Reader,

I am having fun researching and writing the Pony Pal books. I've met great kids and wonderful ponies at homes, farms, and riding schools. Some of my ideas for Pony Pal adventures have even come from these visits.

I remember the day I made up the main characters for the series. I was walking on a country road in New England. First, I decided that the three girls would be smart, independent, and kind. Then I gave them their names—Pam, Anna, and Lulu. (Look at the initial of each girl's name. See what it spells when you put them together.) Later, I created the three ponies. When I reached home, I turned on my computer and started to write. And I haven't stopped since!

My friends say that I am a little bit like all of the Pony Pals. I am very organized, like Pam. I love nature, like Lulu. But I think that I am most like Anna. I am dyslexic and a good artist, just like her.

Readers often wonder about my life. I live in an apartment in New York City near Central Park and the Museum of Natural History. I enjoy swimming, hiking, painting, and reading. I also love to make up stories. I have been writing novels for children and young adults for more than twenty years! Several of my books have won the Children's Choice Award.

Many Pony Pal readers send me letters, drawings, and photos. I tape them to the wall in my office. They inspire me to write more Pony Pal stories. Thank you very much!

I don't ride anymore and I've never had a pony. But you don't have to ride to love ponies! And you certainly don't need a pony to be a Pony Pal.

Happy Reading,

Jeanne Betancourt

Do you love ponies?
Don't miss this sneak preview
of Pony Pals #34

The Pony and the Lost Swan

"Acorn and I will search from the water side," Lulu told Pam as she dismounted. "You keep searching on the trail side."

Lulu led Acorn into the shallow water. She scanned the other side of the lake through her binoculars.

Suddenly, Acorn pulled on the reins and whinnied.

"What wrong, Acorn?" Lulu asked as she turned to the pony.

Acorn stared at a plastic shopping bag caught in the underbrush. Lulu was surprised that Acorn spooked over a plastic bag. Usually nothing spooked Anna's pony.

"It's only a plastic bag," Lulu told Acorn.

Acorn pulled on the reins again and sniffed. She wanted to go closer to the plastic bag. "Okay," Lulu agreed. "You can check it out. But I'm telling you that it's nothing to be afraid of."

When they reached the underbrush, Acorn whinnied softly. Lulu realized that Acorn wasn't spooked and he wasn't interested in the plastic bag. A swan lay near the bag in the underbrush.

"Pam," Lulu called out. "Acorn found White Feathers."

Pony Pals®

Be a Pony Pal®!

❏ BBC 0-590-48583-0	#1	I Want a Pony	$3.99 US
❏ BBC 0-590-48584-9	#2	A Pony for Keeps	$3.99 US
❏ BBC 0-590-48585-7	#3	A Pony in Trouble	$3.99 US
❏ BBC 0-590-48586-5	#4	Give Me Back My Pony	$3.99 US
❏ BBC 0-590-25244-5	#5	Pony to the Rescue	$3.99 US
❏ BBC 0-590-25245-3	#6	Too Many Ponies	$3.99 US
❏ BBC 0-590-54338-5	#7	Runaway Pony	$3.99 US
❏ BBC 0-590-54339-3	#8	Good-bye Pony	$3.99 US
❏ BBC 0-590-62974-3	#9	The Wild Pony	$3.99 US
❏ BBC 0-590-62975-1	#10	Don't Hurt My Pony	$3.99 US
❏ BBC 0-590-86597-8	#11	Circus Pony	$3.99 US
❏ BBC 0-590-86598-6	#12	Keep Out, Pony!	$3.99 US
❏ BBC 0-590-86600-1	#13	The Girl Who Hated Ponies	$3.99 US
❏ BBC 0-590-86601-X	#14	Pony-Sitters	$3.99 US
❏ BBC 0-590-86632-X	#15	The Blind Pony	$3.99 US
❏ BBC 0-590-37459-1	#16	The Missing Pony Pal	$3.99 US
❏ BBC 0-590-37460-5	#17	Detective Pony	$3.99 US
❏ BBC 0-590-51295-1	#18	The Saddest Pony	$3.99 US
❏ BBC 0-590-63397-X	#19	Moving Pony	$3.99 US
❏ BBC 0-590-63401-1	#20	Stolen Ponies	$3.99 US
❏ BBC 0-590-63405-4	#21	The Winning Pony	$3.99 US
❏ BBC 0-439-06488-0	#22	The Western Pony	$3.99 US
❏ BBC 0-439-06489-9	#23	The Pony and the Bear	$3.99 US
❏ BBC 0-439-06490-2	#24	Unlucky Pony	$3.99 US
❏ BBC 0-439-06491-0	#25	The Lonely Pony	$3.99 US
❏ BBC 0-439-06492-9	#26	Movie Star Pony	$3.99 US
❏ BBC 0-439-21639-7	#27	The Pony and the Missing Dog	$3.99 US
❏ BBC 0-439-16571-7	#28	The Newborn Pony	$3.99 US
❏ BBC 0-439-16572-5	#29	Lost and Found Pony	$3.99 US
❏ BBC 0-439-16573-3	#30	Pony-4-Sale	$3.99 US
❏ BBC 0-439-21640-0	#31	Ponies from the Past	$3.99 US
❏ BBC 0-439-21641-9	#32	He's My Pony	$3.99 US
❏ BBC 0-439-30642-6	#33	What's Wrong with My Pony?	$3.99 US
❏ BBC 0-590-74210-8		Pony Pals Super Special #1: The Baby Pony	$5.99 US
❏ BBC 0-590-86631-1		Pony Pals Super Special #2: The Story of Our Ponies	$5.99 US
❏ BBC 0-590-37461-3		Pony Pals Super Special #3: The Ghost Pony	$5.99 US
❏ BBC 0-439-30643-4		Pony Pals Super Special #4: The Fourth Pony Pal	$5.99 US

Available wherever you buy books, or use this order form.

Send orders to Scholastic Inc., P.O. Box 7500, Jefferson City, MO 65102

Please send me the books I have checked above. I am enclosing $_____ (please add $2.00 to cover shipping and handling). Send check or money order — no cash or C.O.D.s please.

Please allow four to six weeks for delivery. Offer good in the U.S.A. only. Sorry, mail orders are not available to residents of Canada. Prices subject to change.

Name_____ Birth Date ____/____/____

First   Last   M   D   Y

Address_____

City_____State_____Zip_____

Telephone (   )_____ ❏ Boy   ❏ Girl

Where did you buy this book?   ❏ Bookstore   ❏ Book Fair   ❏ Book Club   ❏ Other   PP701